Thanksgiving Mice!

Thanksgiving Mice!

by Bethany Roberts

illustrated by Doug Cushman

The Library of Congress has cataloged the hardcover edition as follows:
Roberts, Bethany.
Thankgiving mice!/by Bethany Roberts; illustrated by Doug Cushman.
p. cm.
Summary: A group of mice have some problems when they put on a play to
commemorate the first Thanksgiving, but everything works out in the end.
[1. Mice—Fiction. 2. Thanksgiving Day—Fiction. 3. Theater—Fiction.
4. Stories in rhyme.]
I. Cushman, Doug, ill. II. Title.
PZ8.3.R5295 Th 2001
[E]—21   00-047456

ISBN: 978-0-618-12040-6 hardcover
ISBN: 978-0-618-60486-9 paperback
ISBN: 978-0-544-34124-1 GLR paperback
ISBN: 978-0-544-34101-2 GLR paper over board

Manufactured in China
SCP 10 9 8 7 6 5 4 3 2 1

4500473808

Thanksgiving mice
get ready for a show.

Costumes! Sets!
Go, go, go!

Practice lines!
Curtains! Props!

Hurry, hurry!
Oh, no, no!

Thanksgiving mice
shout, "Have a seat!"

"Come one, come all!
Come see our play!"

Pilgrim mice sailed on a ship.

They came from England, far away.

"Raise the anchor!"
"Set the sails!"

"To America we go!"

For many days the Pilgrim mice
in stormy seas tossed to and fro.

They huddled, seasick, in the hold,
hungry, thirsty, filled with dread.

At last their journey
came to an end.

The mice all shouted,
"Land ahead!"

They built new homes in tree trunks,
but felt too weak to sing.

For they were hungry, thin, and cold,

so they waited for the spring.

One day they met some friendly folks,
who gave them corn to sow.

They planted it and tended it,

and watched it grow and grow!

"Thanks to God!"
the mice all squeaked.

"We've lots to eat!
Hooray!"

And so they said
to their new friends,

"Let's feast! Let's dance!
Let's play!"

Thanksgiving mice all take a bow.

Clap! Clap! Clap!
Hurrah! Hooray!

"Come one, come all,
come feast with us—
on this Thanksgiving Day!"